The Little Bitty Bakery

by Leslie Muir • pictures by Betsy Lewin

Disney • Hyperion Books
New York

For Steve and Missy, with love
And to Mom and sweet memories . . .
—L.M.

In loving memory of Ethel Fulton,
the best little bitty baker ever
—B.L.

Text copyright © 2011 by Leslie Muir
Illustrations copyright © 2011 by Betsy Lewin

Publisher's Note: The recipes contained in this book are to be followed exactly as
written, under adult supervision. The Publisher is not responsible for your specific
health or allergy needs that may require medical supervision. The Publisher is not
responsible for any adverse reactions to the recipes contained in this book.

First Edition
10 9 8 7 6 5 4 3 2 1
F850-6835-5-11135
Printed in Singapore

Library of Congress Cataloging-in-Publication Data

Muir, Leslie.
  The little bitty bakery / by Leslie Muir ; illustrations by Betsy
Lewin.—1st ed.
    p. cm.
  Summary: When a pastry chef works straight through her birthday with
no time for birthday cake, some industrious mice make good use of her
kitchen and bake a delicious surprise.
  ISBN 978-1-4231-1640-0 (hardcover)
  [1. Stories in rhyme. 2. Bakers and bakeries—Fiction. 3.
Mice—Fiction. 4. Birthdays—Fiction. 5. Cake—Fiction.] I. Lewin,
Betsy, ill. II. Title.
  PZ8.3.M9223Li 2011
  [E]—dc22   2011012267

Reinforced binding
Hand lettering by Leah Palmer Preiss
Book design by Whitney Manger
Visit www.disneyhyperionbooks.com

At the Little Bitty Bakery,
the pastry chef was beat—
from her powder-sugared nose
to her flour-dusted feet.

She cut the day's last cookie,
checked her custard twice,
bid good night to far-off France,
left cheesecake for the mice.

But as she hung her apron,
her heart began to ache:
"I've worked away my special day.
I've had no birthday cake!"

"It's too late to celebrate,"
she sighed, and climbed in bed—
leaving cookies on the counter,
éclairs*, and raisin bread.

*a long, narrow pastry filled with custard

Her rolling pin lay quiet,
retired for the night.
The whisks and spoons and macaroons
were iced with pale moonlight.

Soon a rustling stir began
behind a sugar bin.
Two ears appeared around the side,
pink and wafer thin.

Then a pair of eyes peeped out
and stole a little stare.
A nose as soft as angel cake
sniffed the sweetened air.

When it seemed the coast was clear,
Mouse *ting*'d a timer chime,
and soon came four more mouse *amis**
in record scurry-time.

*friends

They scuttled to a huddle,
prepared a secret plan,
and launched a luscious mission
inside a brioche* pan.

*fluffy French bread made with lots of eggs and butter

They gathered tumbled crumbles,
bits of sweet delights,
grabbed raisins by their wrinkles,
but never snuck a bite.

They rustled up a hazelnut
and in a dash of time,
fetched rainbow sprinkles on the run,
a wheel of candied lime.

A dainty curl of chocolate
was borrowed last of all;
it topped a most amazing mound
that rose up five-mice tall.

They measured all their morsels
into a custard cup,
threw in a pinch of cinnamon,
then beat a quail egg up.

They shoved it in the oven
with tiny heaves and ho's.
The rack gave way with one loud *SCREEEECH*—
and, like sorbet*, they froze!

*frozen dessert made with fruit

A bedspring creaked and settled
as swirls of sweetness rose
and spiraled to the second floor—
right in the chef's trained nose.

Her eyelids flitter-fluttered.
She smiled a little bit:
"This dream smells sweet as crème brûlée* . . .
but *who* is baking it?"

*rich custard with a hard layer of caramel

She

    tiptoed

       down

          the staircase,

as quiet as a cat—
clutched a day-old stick of bread
just like a baseball bat.

She burst into the kitchen.
Mice scattered to and fro.
They dove into the mixing bowls;
one fell in cookie dough!

The stove was batter splattered.
Meringue peaked from a drawer.
The chef stepped on a butter pat
and slid across the floor.

She came in for a landing
before a dazzling treat.
It towered like a chef's hat
and teetered on mice feet.

The tip-top blazed with candles.
The icing read, SURPRISE!
The mice tossed sprinkles in the air!
Chef's eyes grew round as pies!

She tried a lovely forkful.
Was that a hint of pear?
Or was it chocolate macaroon?
Or coconut éclair?

She took a taste from one end,
a sampling from the other.
This was a crumble jumble cake!
No bite was like another!

She asked the mice to join her.
A twinkle lit her eyes.
"You've brightened up my birthday
with this jumbled-up surprise!"

They had a celebration
and nibbled cake till dawn.
When they set their napkins down,
every crumb was gone.

At the Little Bitty Bakery,
before each morning breaks,
now five wee bakers fill the shelves
with Crumble Jumble cakes!

Crumble Jumble Cake

Heat your oven to 325°.

You'll need:

1 stick unsalted butter (room temperature)
¾ cup sugar
5 large eggs
1 cup chocolate syrup
1 teaspoon pure vanilla extract
⅛ teaspoon cinnamon (optional)
Pinch of salt
1 cup flour

With an electric mixer, cream the butter and sugar until smooth.
Beat in the eggs one at a time. Blend in the chocolate syrup, vanilla extract,
cinnamon, and salt. Add the flour until just combined. Don't overbeat!

Pour the batter into a 9-inch-square nonstick cake pan. Bake for 45 minutes.
Pierce the middle with the point of a knife. If the knife comes out clean, it's done!
Let your cake sit for 15 minutes, then slide it out of the pan onto a cooling rack.
Cool completely. Ice with Moonlight Frosting.

Moonlight Frosting*

Whip together until well combined:

1 stick butter, salted this time (room temperature)
¾ cup powdered sugar
6 tablespoons Marshmallow Fluff
1 teaspoon vanilla extract
1–2 tablespoons half-and-half (to thin)

*Or use your own favorite homemade or store-bought icing!

Jumble Crumbles

When your cake is iced, top with a jumble of crumbles.
Here are a few suggestions from the mice,
but use your imagination!

Chocolate shavings or curls • Cookie crumbles • Raisins
Jelly beans • Coconut • Sprinkles • Berries
Mini chocolate chips • Chopped nuts • Coconut